CRAZY CLASSROOM JOKES AND RIDDLES

NEIL YAMAMOTO

TOR

A TOM DOHERTY ASSOCIATES BOOK
NEW YORK

CRAZY CLASSROOM JOKES AND RIDDLES

Copyright © 1989 by RGA Publishing Group, Inc.

A TOR Book
Published by Tom Doherty Associates, Inc.
49 West 24 Street
New York, NY 10010

ISBN: 0-812-59377-4   Can. ISBN: 0-812-59378-2

First edition: August 1989

Printed in the United States of America

0 9 8 7 6 5 4 3 2 1

Why was the math book sad?
  It had too many problems.

Teacher: *If you worked for ten hours and*
         were paid five dollars an hour,
         what would you get?
Claire: A new dress!

What did the pencil say to the paper?
  "I dot my eyes on you!"

Teacher: *What kind of shape do you think the world is in?*
Patrick: It's round.

Teacher: *What kind of rocks look alike?*
Sandy: Xerox.

*Why did the teacher let the little firefly leave
the room?*
>Because when you have to glow,
>you have to glow.

*Why did the absent-minded student put glue
on his head?*
>Because he thought it would help things
>stick.

When is a teacher like a bird of prey?
 When she watches you like a hawk.

What is a drop of seawater after it
graduates from school?
 Fit to be tide.

How do you begin a book about ducks?
 With the intro-duck-tion.

Younger student: *Is our school haunted?*
Older student: *What makes you ask that?*
Younger student: Well, I keep hearing
    people talking about school spirit.

Why did the elephant do well in school?
    It had a lot of grey matter.

Teacher: *How many minutes are there in an hour?*

Student: 60.

Teacher: *Good. How many seconds in a minute?*

Student: 60.

Teacher: *Correct. Now for a hard one. How many seconds in a year?*

Student: 12.

Teacher: *12?*

Student: Yep. January 2nd, February 2nd, March 2nd....

What is the smallest room in school?
Room for error.

What should you do if your dog eats your
homework?
     Take the words right out of his mouth.

Teacher: *Bill, go to the map and find*
            North America.
Bill: Here it is.
Teacher: *Very good. Now, Class, who*
            discovered North America?
Class: Bill!

Why did the teacher marry the janitor?
Because he swept her off her feet.

What kind of tree does a math teacher climb?
   Geome-tree.

Teacher: *If "can't" is short for "cannot,"*
          what is "don't" short for?
Cassie:: Doughnut.

Why did the music student bring a ladder
to class?
   Because the music teacher asked him
   to sing higher.

Jeff: *How was the history test?*

Nan: Oh, the questions were easy.

Jeff: *Really?*

Nan: Yeah, it was the answers I couldn't get.

Teacher (answering phone): *You say Johnny can't come to school today, because he has a bad cold. To whom am I speaking?*

On the phone: Oh, this is my father.

Teacher: *Janie, what would you do if you saw a man-eating lion?*

Janie: Nothing, because I'm a girl.

When is a child like an animal?
    When they're a teacher's pet.

Define "bacteria."
    The back of a cafeteria.

*What did the student say when the teacher
said, "Order, children, order!"?*
    "I'll have a hamburger and fries, please."

Dad: *How do you like going to school?*
Son: I like going to school and I like coming home from school. It's the time in between I hate.

What happened to the bad egg in the school cafeteria?
    It got egg-spelled.

Father: *Your teacher says you're at the bottom in a class of 20 kids. That's terrible!*

Son: It could be worse.

Father: *How?*

Son: It could be a bigger class.

What kind of food do math teachers eat?
Square meals.

Where's the best place to hide if you're scared?
Inside a math book because there is safety in numbers.

What kind of school has a sign on its door that says, "Please Do Not Knock Before Entering!"?
Karate School.

How would you divide 9 apples between 2 people?
Make applesauce.

What would you get if you crossed a book of nursery rhymes and an orange?
Mother Juice.

Teacher: *How do you spell "scarecrow"?*
Student: S-K-A-R-K-R-O.
Teacher: *That's not how the dictionary spells it.*
Student: You didn't ask me how the dictionary spells it.

Why is a grouchy kindergarten teacher like
a collection of old car parts?
　　She's a crank surrounded by a bunch of
　　little nuts.

What's the difference between a fisherman
and a lazy schoolboy?
　　One baits the hooks, the other hates
　　the books.

Teacher: *Janey, spell "rain".*
Janey: R-A-N-E.
Teacher: That's the worst spell of rain we've
         had around here in a long time.

Why must a school nurse control her temper?
    Because she can't afford to lose her
    patients.

Bill: *How can you be so dumb in school?*
Bob: I practice a lot.

Teacher: *Marion, what can you tell us about the Dead Sea?*

Marion: Gee, I didn't even know it was sick.

Bob: *Are you good at math?*

Rob: Yes and no.

Bob: *What does that mean?*

Rob: Yes, I'm no good at math.

What three R's do cheerleaders learn at school?
    Rah, rah, rah!

Teacher: *What is zinc?*

Student: It's what happens to you when you don't know how to zwim.

Jill: *Our teacher talks to herself.*
Does yours?

Will: Yeah, but she doesn't realize it.
She thinks we're listening.

Bill: *What gives you the most trouble in school?*

Phil: Writing.

Bill: *How come?*

Phil: I can't read.

What do you call a duck who gets straight "A's" on his report card?

A wise quacker.

Why is arithmetic hard work?

All those numerals you have to carry.

Why did the cross-eyed teacher lose his job?
Because he couldn't control his pupils.

Teacher: *Can anyone tell me the longest*
         word in the English language?
Student: S-M-I-L-E-S.
Teacher: *But that only has six letters.*
Student: Sure, but there's a mile between the
         first and last letters.

Teacher: *I hope I didn't see you looking at*
         Don's paper.
Mike: I hope you didn't either.

Teacher: *Why are you late?*

Student: I saw a sign outside that said, "School ahead...Go Slow".

Teacher: *Jeff, can you name something important we didn't have 50 years ago?*

Jeff: Me!

Why wasn't the clock allowed in the classroom?

Because it tocked too much.

What did the computer do in the cafeteria?
  It had a byte.

Friend: *What's your favorite part of school?*
Other Friend: Walking home.

Define the word disease.
  Disease is de grade you get below
  de "B's."

Teacher: Marie, spell mouse.
Marie: M-O-U-S
Teacher: *Isn't there something at the end of it?*
Marie: A tail!

How does a skeleton study for tests?
    He bones up.

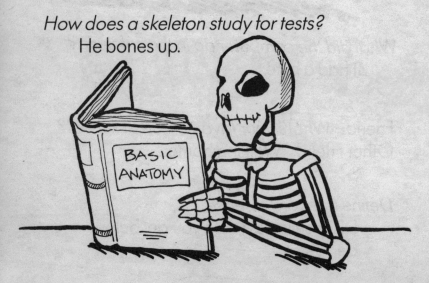

BASIC ANATOMY

Who's the teacher in a ghoul's school?
    The creature teacher.

Teacher: *Yes, Timmy?*
Timmy: I don't want to scare you, but my
         dad said if I didn't get better
         grades, someone is due for a
         spanking.

*Why were the Middle Ages also called the
Dark Ages?*
    Because there were so many knights.

Billy: *Want to play school?*

Willy: Okay, I'll play I'm absent.

Teacher: *What is the definition of ignorance?*

Natalie: Uh, I don't know.

Teacher: Correct!

How can you prevent diseases from biting insects?

Don't bite any.

Why do they say the pen is mightier than the sword?
Because no one has invented the ball point sword.

Teacher: *Will, how do you spell Mississippi?*
Will: The river or the state?

What comes before March?
Forward!

Name five things that contain milk.
Ice cream, cheese, and three cows.

Teacher: *Jon, why is your report on milk so short?*

Jon: I wrote about condensed milk.

Teacher: *Andy, what is a vacuum?*

Andy: I'm not sure, but my father says I have one inside my head.

What does an elf do when it gets home from school?

It's gnomework.

Where do children grow?
 In a kinder-garden.

What's the difference between a school bus driver and a cold?
 One knows the stops and the other stops the nose.

How do bees get to school?
 By school buzz.

What kinds of tests do witches take?
Hex-aminations.

Why are students' grades so low after the holidays?
Well, you know how everything gets marked down after Christmas…

Where do vampires learn to read?
Ghoul school.

Son: *Dad, I just saved you some money!*
Dad: How did you do that?
Son: *I won't need new books next year.*
      I'm taking the same classes again.

Bill: *Where are you taking that skunk?*
Will: To school for show and tell.
Bill: *What about the smell?*
Will: Oh, he'll get used to it.

Teacher: *Where is the English Channel?*
Perry: I don't know. I guess my television doesn't pick it up.

Harry: *Do you want to hear about the broken pencil?*
Larry: No, there's no point to it.

Do dogs ever go to school?
Yes, but they always have a "ruff" time.

Why don't owls do well in school?
    They don't give a hoot.

What is the first thing little vampires learn in school?
    The alpha-bat.

Which is smarter, a cabbage or a carrot?
    A cabbage, because it has a head.

Why was the little bird punished at school?
It was caught peeping during a test.

Teacher: *Jimmy, do we get fur from lions?*
Jimmy: Yes, we get as "fur" as possible!

Teacher: *If you add 3426 and 7625, then divide the answer by 3 and multiply by 7, what would you get?*

Student: I'd get the wrong answer.

Teacher: *What do we do with crude oil?*

Nina: Teach it manners.

Why did the student swallow a dollar?
   It was his lunch money.

Teacher: *What are you going to be when you get out of school?*
Bobby: An old man.

Teacher: *Can anyone tell me one use for horse hide?*
Student: To hold the horse together.

Teacher: *Name four members of the insect family.*

Willie: Mother, father, sister, and brother.

Teacher: *What do you call the small rivers that run into the Nile?*

Matt: Juve-niles

Teacher: *What is the center of gravity?*

Steve: The letter "V."

Why didn't the skeleton do well in school?
His heart wasn't in it.

How many months have twenty-eight days in them?

All of them!

What's the best type of food to serve at school?

Alphabet soup.

What's yellow, has wheels, and lies on its back?
     A dead school bus.

Mr. Cooke: *If you study and work hard, you'll get ahead.*

Sam: No thanks. I'm not really using the one I have now.

Mr. Stoltz: *Davey, you're late again. Don't you have a clock that tells time?*

Davey: No, sir. It doesn't know how to talk.

What is the first thing a little snake learns in school?

Hiss-tory.

Teacher: *Ted, I asked you to draw a wagon and a horse. You only drew a horse.*

Ted: I figured the horse would draw the wagon.

What grade hurts the most to get?
    A "B," because it stings.

Parent: *Why aren't you doing well in history class?*
Child: Because the teacher keeps asking me questions about things that happened before I was born.

What is big and yellow and comes in the morning to brighten mother's day?
    The school bus.

What subject do runners like the best?
    Jog-raphy.

What kind of pliers do you use in arithmetic?
    Multi-pliers.

What do history teachers make when they want to get together?
    Dates.

What is the wettest grade you can get?
    A "C" (sea).

Why did the one-eyed monster close down his school?
     Because he had only one pupil.

Parent: *How are you doing in arithmetic?*
Child: I've learned to add up the zeroes, but the numbers still give me trouble.

What is an autobiography?
A car's life story.

Why do dragons always fall asleep in class?
    Because they hunt knights.

On what side of a school does an oak tree grow?
    The outside.

Why is a drama teacher like the pony express?
    Because he's a stage coach.

Two teachers teach at the same school. One is the father of the other's son. What relation are they to each other?
    Husband and wife.

What do you call a person who teaches knitting?
    A knit-wit.

Teacher: *Billy, why do polar bears have fur?*
Billy: Because they'd look funny in
             jackets.

A class has a top and bottom. What lies in between?
    The student body.

What do you get when you cross a science teacher with a tree?
    Albert Pinestein.

Why is school out at 3?
    The bell strikes 1,
    strikes 2,
    strikes 3,
    and you're out!

*How can a teacher tell if there's an elephant
in the classroom?*
    Ask a question; if someone raises a trunk
    instead of a hand, then there's an
    elephant.

*When can you get an entire school under an
umbrella and not get wet?*
    When it's not raining.

What part of a book is like a fish?
     The fin-ish.

What do you get if you cross one principal with another?
     Don't do it. Principals don't like to be crossed.

TAP! TAP! TAP! TAP! TAP!

What do they teach vampires in business courses?
How to type blood.

Why are misers good math teachers?
Because they know how to make every penny count.

What do you get when you cross a dog with a piano teacher?

A dog whose Bach is worse than his bite.

What did the professor say as his glass eye
slid down the drain?
   "I guess I've lost another pupil!"

Where do knights study?
   In knight school.

What is a wisecrack?
    An educated hole-in-the-wall.

Teacher: *What's the difference between*
          electricity and lightning?
Student: We have to pay for electricity.

Teacher: *How many sheep does it take to make one sweater?*

David: None. Sheep can't knit.

Teacher: *Jill, did anyone help you with these math problems?*

Jill: No ma'am. I got them wrong all by myself.

Teacher: *You missed school yesterday, didn't you, Mike?*

Mike: No, not very much.

What animal is the best at math?
 Rabbits; they multiply the fastest.